Ne...

EILEEN GOUDGE

Welcome to
Carson Springs

SIGNET
Published by New American Library, a division of
Penguin Putnam Inc., 375 Hudson Street,
New York, New York 10014, U.S.A.
Penguin Books Ltd, 80 Strand,
London WC2R 0RL, England
Penguin Books Australia Ltd, Ringwood,
Victoria, Australia
Penguin Books Canada Ltd, 10 Alcorn Avenue,
Toronto, Ontario, Canada M4V 3B2
Penguin Books (N.Z.) Ltd, 182–190 Wairau Road,
Auckland 10, New Zealand

Penguin Books Ltd, Registered Offices:
Harmondsworth, Middlesex, England

First published by Signet, an imprint of New American Library,
a division of Penguin Putnam Inc.

First Printing, May 2002
10 9 8 7 6 5 4 3 2 1

Contents

Dear Reader,

I grew up in a small town in California. I remember Saturdays, riding my bike to the library then stopping at the Little Store on my way home for ice cream that came in only two flavors (vanilla and marble fudge) and cost ten cents for a double scoop. This is the world I set out to recreate in the fictional Carson Springs, where the sun shines year round and the only thing juicier than the oranges is the local gossip.

Come on in, don't be shy. Old Clem Woolley, on the park bench with a tattered bundle of his self-published tome, might look a little strange, but he's harmless. And if you spy Sister Agnes, from the beekeeping convent known for its Blessed Bee honey, helping herself to something that doesn't belong to her, your eyes aren't deceiving you (and she's one of the good guys!). Oh, and that glamorous woman in the wheelchair? That's former movie star Monica Vincent, who was crippled in an accident but still manages to stir up plenty of trouble.

Stroll down the street a bit and you'll come to Delarosa's, the general store back in the days of the gold rush, now an arts and crafts emporium run by the widowed Sam Kiley. In *Stranger in Paradise*, forty-eight-year-old Sam, who's recently taken up with her daughter's thirty-year-old stepson, has gone from being a pillar of the community to the talk of the town. The fact that she's pregnant makes it all the more scandalous.

If you want to find out what happens with Sam, her two grown daughters, the mysterious teen runaway Finch, and the serial murderer on the loose in Carson Springs, you won't have long to wait. *Taste of Honey* (due out this June in hardcover), features Sam's best friend, Gerry Fitzgerald, a former nun turned lusty divorcée, who is reunited with the daughter she gave up for adoption nearly thirty years before. Along the way, you'll be reacquainted with your favorite characters from *Stranger in Paradise*, including Sam, who gives birth to a— Oops! I almost gave away the best part.

Can't wait until then? Lucky for you, there's "Heaven on Earth," a little prequel contained herein about Sam's parents and life in Carson Springs back in the fifties—a story I hope will satisfy like a ten-cent double scoop of marble fudge.

I'll also share a little secret with you: My hobby is baking. Those of you who remember Tea & Sympathy from *One Last Dance* will be happy to know it's making a comeback in *Taste of Honey*. If you'd like to see some of the actual recipes you can log on to my Web site: www.eileengoudge.com. I've included two of my favorites here, one of which was shared by a reader. I hope you enjoy them as much as my friends and family have.

And now, I bid you farewell . . . but only for the time being. Remember, Carson Springs is just around the bend. See you there.

Warmly,

Eileen Goudge

Welcome to Carson Springs

HEAVEN ON EARTH

At the highest point on Route 33, just south of Ventura, where it twists up through sandstone bluffs with fanciful names like Moon's Nest and Sleeping Indian Chief, where condors and red-tailed hawks draw the eye heavenward, and it's not unusual to see a snakeskin on the rocks, glimmering like the promise of gold that once drew settlers to these remote hills, the steep grade levels off in a windswept overlook. On it stands a bronze plaque mounted on a rough granite base, its raised lettering blackened but still legible.

THE ACADEMY AWARD–NOMINATED FILM, *Stranger in Paradise* (1958), WAS SHOT ON LOCATION IN CARSON SPRINGS. THE FAMOUS OPENING PANORAMA IS THE VIEW FROM THIS OVERLOOK.

Few even notice it until lured into pulling over by a view so awe-inspiring it might have been an exaggerated version of itself, like the hand-tinted postcards on display at the museum. A deep tureen of a valley, ringed by snowcapped mountains all around—the ancient collision of two transverse ranges—in which divergent geologies bookend the orange groves that run in neat, cross-stitched rows along the verdant floor: at the eastern end, a pristine wooded lake, and at the western, a deserty scrawl of chaparral. The town itself seems almost incidental: a loose cluster of terra-cotta-roofed buildings, presided over by the domed tower of the Coolidge-era post office, its streets bending and looping to accommodate century-old trees no one had the heart to cut down.

Breathe deeply and you'll catch the scent of sage, reminiscent of attic trunks in which sheaves of crumbling letters are stored. Listen closely and you'll hear the chorus of birds: the short, sharp trill of the dark-eyed junco and frenetic *whi-whi-whi* of the white-breasted nuthatch. At sunset on a clear day you'll witness a phenomenon known as the pink moment, when the mountains to the east are bathed in rose-colored light—an occurrence to which locals have attributed almost mystical properties: the time a baby is most likely to be born and a dying man to exhale his final breath. It's been said a marriage proposal made at that moment will result in a lasting union, though no one's ever been able to prove it, since nearly every long-wed couple in Carson Springs claims to have launched their union with the pink light of sunset.

In the mid-eighties, long after *Stranger in Paradise* had drifted into the twilight of late-night television, a white-haired couple could often be seen poised on the overlook at sunset, heads lightly touching, hands entwined like the roots of inter-locking trees. The rose-colored light bathing the distant mountains illuminated their faces as well, lending the fleeting impression of young lovers artificially aged for cinematic purposes. In later years the old woman stood alone, her face tipped to the sky in silent communion, wearing the look of someone reliving events long past. She would stand motionless until the last of the light had faded and evening shadows crept out of hiding. Then she would turn and walk slowly back to her car. Those who knew her from town often recognized her Pontiac before they did her. For high on the ridge, with her skirt fluttering in the breeze, there was something ageless about her, like a frame from what locals referred to simply as The Movie.

Her name was Cora Delarosa, and even when well into her seventies, you could see she'd once been beautiful. In 1957, when a crew from 20th Century Fox descended on Carson Springs like a flock of rare migrating birds, she'd been all of thirty-two and just shy of her twelfth wedding anniversary. In addition to raising eight-year-old Ray and two young daughters, Samantha and Au-drey, she and her husband ran the general store that had been in his family since the days of the gold rush. They attended mass every Sunday, oc-cupying a pew polished by generations of Dela-rosa backsides. Cora sang in the choir as well, a soprano so pure and haunting Father Octavio often imagined it to be an angel's.

Life was good.

Cora, the motherless daughter of a roustabout, had bounced from one place to another before finding a home in Carson Springs. Her husband Jack, a descendant of the valley's earliest Spanish settlers, known as the *gente de razon*, had lived there all his life and seldom set foot outside the valley. They made an odd pair. Jack, with his rangy build top-heavy like a blacksmith's and dark eyes that peered from under a shelf of eyebrow, and swan-necked, auburn-haired Cora, possessed of a natural grace and refined manner. Jack seemed the long shadow cast by his luminous wife. People were aware of it when he entered a room, especially when trouble was brewing. Air charged with static would settle back on its heels; knuckles would loosen and eyes would lower. He had a way of settling matters with a level look or firm clap on the shoulder. Like the night at the Red Rooster Tavern when Joe Hartnell and Everett Gaines were on the verge of going tooth and nail.

"The damn Ruskies have us all runnin' scared," Jack said after Joe had accused Everett of being unpatriotic. "That's no reason for every Tom, Dick, and Harry to be hacking down trees and digging bomb shelters. Hell, dig deep enough and we'll all end up in China."

There were muttered assents and a few uneasy chuckles. Shots of whiskey were poured, and talk turned to other things. That was the way it was with Jack. Men looked up to him, and women wanted him without quite knowing why. Customers walked away feeling they'd gotten fair value for their hard-earned dollar. And in 1952, when the town council pitted itself against the orange growers by proposing a ban on smudge pots, it was Jack to whom the warring factions turned. He'd suggested hiring an expert to conduct a study, whose findings had shown the source of smog to be a fire in neighboring Los Padres national forest.

To Cora he wasn't handsome or ugly, humble or heroic. He was simply her husband. The man she opened her eyes to every morning of the week, three hundred sixty-five days of the year. She never even gave much thought to whether or not she loved him, any more than she would have with her children . . . until one day, in April, when Hank Montgomery stepped into her life through a back door she hadn't even known was ajar.

It was a blustery day with Easter just around the corner. Customers had been blowing in and out all morning, bringing gusts of mild spring air. Shortly before closing time the bell over the door tinkled, and she looked up to find a stocky, fair-haired man striding toward her.

"Mrs. Delarosa?" He stuck out a large, callous hand, and she looked into a face that matched his handshake: firm and to the point. "Hank Montgomery, from Twentieth Century Fox. I'm directing the picture you may have heard about."

She felt a light chill tiptoe up her spin. Who hadn't heard of it? The Movie was all anyone had talked about for weeks. In a day when movies were usually shot on back lots, a film crew might have been a circus come to town. There'd been talk of the caravan parked up on Sleeping Indian

Chief, of fast-talking men and flashy women, of
two-dollar tips and parties that went on all night
out at the Horse Creek Inn. Billy Soper claimed to
have spotted Selma Lamb riding a bicycle along
Agua Caliente Road, though Elroy Beese said it
had to have been her double. And Mary Ellen
Riggs, down at the Blue Bonnet Café, had saved
the butt from Burke Howard's cigarette, which she
was planning to have bronzed.

Cora was determined not to succumb to such
silliness. Even with her heart racing, she asked
politely and somewhat coolly, "What can I do for
you, Mr. Montgomery?"

"Hank, please." His blue eyes crinkled in a
smile so full of warmth and merry promise it was
like an invitation to some exclusive event. "One
of my men was in a few weeks ago. Curt McGar-
rity, our location scout. He spoke with . . . your
husband, I believe it was?"

Cora struggled to keep her surprise from showing. "I'm sorry. He didn't mention it to me. It
must have slipped his mind," she said. "Is there
anything I can help you with?"

"We'd like to use your store as a backdrop for
one of the scenes," Hank replied as if it were a
pound of coffee, or a bag of nails, he was asking
for.

Cora, thunderstruck, glanced about at the laby-
rinthian aisles and crowded shelves. The store,
like the town itself, had grown out of necessity
rather than some overall plan. Staples and feed
and farm implements had burgeoned to include
kitchenware and crockery and fabrics by the yard.

They sold Jell-O molds, biscuit cutters, splatter-ware coffeepots and canisters, even specialty items like the honey bottled by the nuns of Our Lady of the Wayside, and oranges in crates for tourists to take home. A row of jars on the counter held an array of sweets, from sour balls to licorice whips, and in the morning there were doughnuts from Ingersoll's.

"Goodness," she said.

Hank was quick to reassure her. "All we need is some footage of the exterior, with a shot of Selma walking out the door. It wouldn't take more than a few hours. We'd film on Sunday when you're closed."

"I'll have to speak with my husband," she said, more than a little annoyed at Jack for not telling her.

Hank, who looked to be in his forties, with the rugged appearance of someone who spent a great deal of time outdoors, leaned an elbow onto the counter and spoke confidingly. "Look, I'll be honest with you, Mrs. Delarosa. I'm more used to telling people what to do than I am at asking nicely. So if I'm not doing any better of a job persuading you than my man Curt, just tell me and I'll be on my way." He didn't have to say it: There were other stores.

"Oh, it's not that," she said, torn between loyalty to Jack and a desire to leap at this golden opportunity. "It's just . . . I don't know what my husband will say."

Jack usually resisted anything new. It had taken months to convince him to trade in their old station wagon for the new Rambler he was at this very moment picking up at the dealer's. He'd argued that they couldn't afford it, which was only partly true. Though they owned land granted to his great-grandfather by the king of Spain, land worth hundreds of thousands, he would sooner cut off a big toe than part with so much as a square foot.

"Maybe if I spoke with him myself . . . ?" Hank glanced about as if half expecting to see Jack amid the shelves in back.

"I'm afraid he's not here." She hesitated before adding, "Why don't you come back tomorrow? We open at nine."

"Nine it is." He tipped her a little salute, smiling that irresistible smile, his eyes like chinks of blue sky glinting through weathered boards.

He was halfway to the door before she remembered to ask, "Where are you staying? In—in case we need to reach you."

He turned to face her, absently patting the pocket of his khaki shirt, where she could see the outline of his cigarettes. "Horse Creek Inn," he told her. "It's not fancy, but for us rough-and-tumble folk it'll do." He winked knowingly, and she wondered if he'd caught wind of the gossip. Ruth Anne Wilcox, at the post office, had stated authoritatively that everyone in Hollywood hopped in and out of beds like Mexican jumping beans, and the crew up at the inn was no exception. "Oh, by the way, any place around here I can get a decent meal? Haven't had much luck so far."

"Miller's isn't bad," she said, pointing out the window at the café catty-corner to Delarosa's. "For breakfast, there's Ingersoll's. You've never tasted buttermilk crullers until you've tried Helga's. Make a left on Old Mission. It's two blocks down on your right."

"Thanks." He dug a cigarette from his pocket. "Stop by on your way to work tomorrow," he said. "I'll buy you a cup of coffee and one of those crullers."

Her cheeks grew warm, but just as she was about to say she didn't think her husband would approve, she thought better of it. Surely he'd meant for the invitation to include Jack as well. Jack, for whom the very idea would be as unthinkable as a trip to the moon.

Cora was seized by a sudden recklessness. "I just may take you up on that."

"It'd be an honor." Hank gave a courtly little bow. "A pleasure meeting you, Mrs. Delarosa."

"Cora," she said.

"Cora," he repeated as if the name were a secret she'd shared.

He stepped out the door, and she watched through the window as he set off across the plaza, striding purposefully like a man used to getting his way. She felt light-headed and a bit unsteady, as if she'd stepped off a boat and hadn't quite gotten her bearings. Anyone glancing in would have seen a slender, auburn-haired woman poised as if in thought, absently fingering the locket at her throat. Those used to seeing her bustling about or teetering on tiptoe to reach a high shelf would have wondered what had given her pause. It was a minute or so before she shook her head as if to clear it, then walked over to flip the sign on the door.

A few minutes later, precisely at five, she stepped outside to lock up. The plaza was nearly deserted, only a few weary shoppers sipping sodas at the tables in front of Miller's Café. Herb Miller, a World War I veteran who'd lost a leg in Antibes and was prone when emphasizing a point to unstrapping his prosthetic and thumping it down in front of the startled dissenter, stumped out to greet her.

"Howdy, Missus." He always addressed her in that manner, never Mrs. Delarosa, or heaven forbid, Cora.

"Evening, Mr. Miller. How's business?"

"Can't complain." It was his standard response, though in her opinion the place could use some freshening up—a new awning, a coat of white-wash, some window boxes maybe. Like her husband, Herb Miller would just as soon see the whole town pickled in brine. His brows—a heavy black that contrasted startlingly with the snowy hair that drifted about his head—drew together in a frown. "That one of them Hollywood folk I seen a bit ago?"

"As a matter of fact, it was."

He made a harrumphing sound. "No respect for decent folk, that bunch. Why, one of 'em come sniffin' round Rose the other day. Or was it Olive?" He scratched his head, looking confused.

Cora pressed her lips together in an effort to keep from smiling. The Miller twins, Olive and Rose, had had the misfortune of being born not only homely but as a matched set, poor things. Only Rose had been lucky enough to find a husband.

"I'll be on my guard," she said with the utmost solemnity. "Good evening, Mr. Miller. Give my best to the girls." Mrs. Miller had been dead for some years, and it was Olive and Rose (at thirty, no longer girls) who helped run the café.

As she made her way across the plaza, Cora imagined how it would look on a ten-foot movie screen—its graceful Spanish storefronts and pretty tiled fountain, its adobe walls festooned in bougainvillea. She glanced up at the arch, where DELA-ROSA PLAZA was spelled out in decorative tiles. She remembered the first time she'd walked through that arch as a bride, how humbled she'd felt seeing Jack's name up there—*her* name now. More than a decade later it still gave her a deep sense of belonging, the feeling of having been blown like a seed from dry topsoil to a place where she could at last sink roots.

Stepping onto the street, she started up the covered arcade that stretched along the south side of Old Mission to Calle de Navidad. With dinner hour approaching, pedestrians were few and far between. The swallows nesting in the rafters overhead swooped in and out of view, calling raucously to one another. Across from the park, she could see the church steeple of the mission peek-

ing up over the treetops. The pealing of its campanile bells—the bell choir practicing for Easter
services—was soothing and familiar.

No sooner had she crossed the street than a
shiny new Rambler, dark green with beige trim,
pulled up to the curb. Jack rolled his window
down and stuck his head out. "Hey, lady. Need
a lift?"

"If it's not out of your way," Cora replied,
straight-faced. Primly, she walked around to the
passenger side and got in.

"What do you think? Isn't she a beauty?" Jack
tooted the horn, causing a few pedestrians to cast
startled looks over their shoulders. "And hey, listen to this." He turned a knob on the dash, and
the pealing of the campanile bells was at once
drowned out by Pat Boone crooning, "Ain't That
a Shame."

"Did Mr. Baxter give you a fair trade on the
Pontiac?"

"Two hundred, and he threw in a set of white-
walls." Jack looked as pleased as their eight-year-
old when Ray landed a bull's-eye with his sling-
shot. You'd never have known the car was her
idea.

"That's more than I expected."

He'd been to the barber that morning and his
wiry black hair was slicked into neat waves. He
might as well not have bothered with the shave;
his jaw was already shadowed with stubble. She
wondered if he would shave before bed tonight.
It was his unspoken signal: When she saw Jack's

razor on the bathroom sink she knew to put in
her diaphragm.

Cora found herself blushing as she always did
when such thoughts came upon her in broad day-
light. As if people could peek into her mind the
way they could into the window of her shop.
What, she wondered, would they have thought?
Were she and Jack different from other couples?
She had no way of knowing. Jack was the only
man she'd even been with.

They drove slowly past the post office, with
its bell tower that tolled the hour, day in and
day out—a reminder of all that was steady, mea-
sured, enduring. Not much had changed since
Cora had first come here, except that the old
playhouse had been converted into a movie theatre dubbed the Park Rio. A year ago last June,
when the planning commission approved a de-
velopment that would turn the old Weedman
ranch into Carson Springs's first subdivision,
Jack had spoken out against it at a town council
meeting for which half the town turned out.
Luckily, he'd prevailed.

"Someone stopped by while you were out, the
director of that picture." She spoke with deliberate
casualness. "He said one of his men had spoken
to you a few weeks back."

Jack shrugged as if it were more of an annoy-
ance than anything. "Sure, I remember. Young fel-
low, cocky as all get-out. Had this crazy idea of
putting us in their movie. Can you believe it?"

"What did you tell him?"

He shot her a surprised look. "That we weren't interested. What else?"

Cora could no longer contain herself. "Oh, Jack. What would be the harm in it? For heaven's sake, this is the most exciting thing that's happened to us in years!"

He gave a snort of derision. "That's what my uncle Joe said when he ran off to make his fame and fortune in Hollywood. Last we heard of him . . . until he showed up two years later in the drunk tank."

"Your uncle would have ended up there anyway," she argued.

"Maybe, maybe not." All the new-car joy had gone out of his face. His expression was dark and preoccupied.

They'd left the downtown area and were making their way along Grove Avenue, with its neat rows of orange trees behind low stone walls as far as the eye could see. She felt chilled all of a sudden, even with the mild spring air blowing in through the open windows. "Jack, it wouldn't kill us to—"

"What would our customers think?"

"They might think it was cute."

"Cute isn't what sells, Cora."

She looked around her. At the shiny dashboard and tan plush ceiling; at the spotless rubber mat on which her flat-heeled shoes rested. She felt all at once defeated. "It was just a thought," she said.

Cora stared silently out the window. The road grew steeper and more winding. Citrus groves gave way to strands of eucalyptus and pepper. Along the shoulder, wildflowers shouted from the ditches—golden yarrow and chicory, monkey flower, great clumps of Matilija poppies bursting with white blossoms. Beyond, trails worn into grooves by horses' hooves led back into the trees.

Then they were climbing the hill to Isla Verde. As their house rose above the treetops—two stories of cream-colored adobe roofed in terra-cotta, with a pair of round towers like silos flanking the courtyard in front—she thought, *I should be grateful for what I have.* Growing up, she hadn't even had indoor plumbing. What was a silly movie compared to all this?

Inside, the girls rushed to greet her, nearly tripping over each other in an effort to get there first. Four-year-old Audrey held up a crayon drawing for her to admire. "Mami, look what I drew!"

"Very pretty." She bent to examine it. "Is that a horse?"

Audrey shook her head, looking vaguely put out.

"It's Buttons," her sister put in helpfully. Sam, who was six going on sixteen. "See, that's his collar."

"So it is." Cora could hear their golden retriever in the backyard barking at some poor, treed creature. She straightened and looked around. "Where's your brother?"

"He spilled his milk," Audrey announced in a superior tone. "Lupe's making him clean it up."

Of all the children she looked the most like Jack, with her wiry black hair and small dark eyes that peered fiercely from under a single black eyebrow. Cora sighed inwardly. Her younger daughter was the most difficult of her three children. Always needing to be first at everything, and sulking when she wasn't the center of attention. Even at her birth—a long and especially arduous one— Audrey had emerged red-faced and scowling, as if challenging Cora to love her.

"Well, go get him. Poppi's taking you all for a drive in the new car." Cora flapped a hand in the direction of the kitchen.

Audrey raced off to find her brother, crying loudly, "I get to sit in front!"

Sam just stood there, her small face troubled. "What's the matter, Mami?" She peered up at Cora with solemn gray-green eyes.

Cora started, then smiled. It wasn't the first time Sam had sensed something wrong. They were so much alike, she might have been Cora at that age. Both were slender and small-boned, with narrow hands and feet, and dark auburn hair that wouldn't hold a curl. Sam shared her tendency to take things to heart as well.

Cora bent to hug Sam, who smelled faintly of whatever spicy dish their housekeeper was preparing. "Nothing's the matter," she said. "Now run along. Poppi's waiting."

Twenty minutes later they were back from their ride, so excited she could hardly get them to sit down at the table. Jack had promised to take them to Palisades Park on Sunday, and it was all they could talk about over supper. Ray, the image of Cora's burly roustabout father, right down to the gap between his front teeth, begged to go on the roller coaster. When Jack informed him that he'd have to grow at least two more inches before he'd be allowed on, he howled in protest. Jack put an end to it by bringing up something he'd read in today's paper.

"Doctors are saying you can get cancer from smoking," he said, lighting up a Pall Mall. "I wonder if there's anything to it."

His razor wasn't on the bathroom sink when it came time for bed. As Cora slipped in next to him, he only kissed her on the cheek before rolling over to switch off the lamp. Long after he began to snore, she lay awake, memories stealing through the dark to catch her about the throat.

The war was still on in the Pacific when they met, at a canteen near Fort Roberts, where he'd trained. He'd been standing by the door with a group of his buddies, smoking a cigarette. Not the best-looking soldier there, but something about him drew her gaze. Maybe it was the snug fit of his khaki uniform, or the confidence in every line of his rangy, bull-necked body slouched up against the wall. The kind of man, she thought, who'd be the first to put his hand up at a grange hall or union meeting . . . and the first to get shot charging an enemy line. She grew frightened at the idea, though that was silly—she didn't even know his name. It wasn't until halfway through the evening, when he asked her to dance, that she learned he was shipping out the following day.

"Will you write?" His eyes searched hers as they swayed to "Moonlight Serenade."

"That depends," she said, a little shocked by the abruptness of his request.

"On what?"

"On whether you'll write me back." She'd tilted her head coyly, but looking into his eyes she saw that he was serious. An electric thrill shot through her, leaving her weak-kneed.

"I'd be a fool not to," he said.

"In that case, write me first."

He smiled at her as if at some wild horse he'd managed to corral, which he now had to figure out what to do with, as she scribbled her address inside a matchbook. When she handed it to him, he said, "I'll bet you think this was what I was after all along."

She laughed. "Well, wasn't it?"

He looked at her long and hard, and there was something in his gaze that made her tremble inside. "It'd mean a lot," he said, "having something to look forward to." His tone made it clear he was referring to more than letters.

Cora often wondered what would have become of them had it not been for those letters. Letters that grew more heartfelt as the war in the Pacific dragged on. Like wives and girlfriends everywhere, she began to live in fear of the telegram that might come instead. In the tense months before victory was declared, she followed his battalion's progress with a fervent hope once reserved for the mother who'd walked out on her and her father when Cora was ten. She knew her mother wasn't ever coming back, but prayed that Jack would.

When he returned home at last, gaunt and yellow from malaria, but mercifully intact, she tearfully accepted his proposal. Three months later, they were married at St. Xavier's, and she moved into Isla Verde, where Jack lived with his widowed mother. Jack's father had died some years back, but Pilar Delarosa—a flinty, fierce-eyed woman for whom Cora developed a grudging affection—had clung tenaciously to life despite a severe heart ailment. She wouldn't leave this earth, she said, until she'd laid eyes on her first grandchild. Three days after Ray's christening, Jack and his sister, Florine, were burying her in the cemetery up on Pilgrim's Mount.

I'm thirty-two and I feel sixty, she thought as she lay in the dark, tears slipping down her temples into her hair. What had happened to her shy, but eager bridegroom, the soldier who'd battled his way through the jungles of Corregidor with her photo pressed to his heart? When had he become this dull man in pajamas who no longer reached for her in the night? A man who, these days, appeared to take as little pleasure from the act as he gave.

The following morning Cora dressed carefully. On the way to work, Jack let her off in front of Ingersoll's, where every morning she picked up their standing order of six dozen doughnuts. "Don't wait," she told him. "I have a couple of errands to run. I'll meet you back at the shop."

It wasn't exactly a lie—she *did* have to stop at the drugstore to pick up that prescription for Audrey's eczema—but she felt a stab of guilt nonetheless. Which was only compounded when Jack

said sweetly, "Take your time." He was trying to
make up for yesterday, she knew, and she was
touched when he caught her hand, giving it a little squeeze.

Inside, the bakery was fragrant and the glass
case in front lightly fogged. A line of customers
spilled over into the café in back. Helga Ingersoll, a large woman with pale hair in a bun and
a face permanently flushed from trying to keep
up with demands, manned the register while the
eldest of her three daughters filled orders. Cora
noted the pink box marked "Delarosa" on a
shelf behind the counter.

"Cora?"

Cora glanced about, nearly bumping into
Gladys Moore, on her way out the door with her
young daughter, Marguerite, in tow. Her heart
sank. The last person on earth she wanted to see.

"Gladys . . . hi." She smiled at Marguerite, who
was in Sam's first grade class. "What's that you've
got there?"

Marguerite was clutching a bulging bag as if it
were an armful of kittens that might get away.
She said brightly, "Mommy said I could hold it if
I promise not to eat any."

Gladys, president of St. Xavier's altar guild,
was the one who'd shot down Cora's suggestion
of using wildflowers in this year's Easter display. Marguerite, nearly as plump as her
mother, could have used the same firm hand
when it came to doling out sweets, Cora
thought.

Gladys flashed her an insincere smile. "This is

such a coincidence. I was just on my way to see you."

Cora arranged her features in a bright look. "Oh?"

"We missed you at last Tuesday's meeting." Gladys dropped her voice to add, "I was worried you might be under the weather."

Cora felt herself flush. She was one of the few parish wives who worked outside the home, and Gladys never missed an opportunity to remind her. "We were taking inventory that night," she replied sweetly. "Why don't you save me a copy of the minutes?"

Gladys's smile faded. "Yes, of course."

Cora breathed a sigh of relief when they disappeared out the door. She was making her way toward the back, hoping she hadn't missed Hank, when she ran into Mavis Fitzgerald. Her daughter, Gerry, was Sam's best friend in school and the two mothers had hit it off as well.

"Well, look at you, smart as a new dollar bill." Mavis's voice still carried a touch of an Irish lilt. She pushed a hand through hair that was rusty where Cora's was a deep, almost mahogany red. "And just who is the lucky mister? Your husband, I hope." Her green eyes danced with merriment.

Blood surged up into Cora's cheeks. But Mavis was only teasing; she couldn't possibly know about Hank. "Speaking of husbands, how's Frank?"

"Oh, you know . . . we take it day by day." Mavis spoke lightly. Even with her husband so ill, she seemed determined to remain upbeat. But some of the light had gone out of her freckled face even so. Cora wished there was some way she could help.

She touched Mavis's arm. "If you need anything, just let me know."

Mavis smiled sadly, and Cora felt suddenly shallow and greedy. What wouldn't Mavis have given for her husband to be healthy and whole again?

"See you on Sunday," she called to Cora on her way out. Mavis never missed mass.

Cora found Hank at a table in back, smoking a cigarette and leafing through the *Clarion*. He glanced up at her, a look of pleasant surprise spreading across his tanned, rugged face.

"I'd just about given up on you," he said, rising to his feet.

"I'm here every morning at the same time," she said, hoping he wouldn't guess the truth: that she never stayed longer than it took to ring up her order. The table was so close to the wall, she had to squeeze past him to get to the other chair. It might as well have been her bare skin brushing against his.

"Cigarette?" Hank held out a crumpled pack.

"No, thanks. I don't smoke." At the moment it weas all she could do just to catch her breath.

"Well, I owe you a cup of coffee at least." He signaled to the waitress. From the kitchen in back came the clatter of pans, the sizzle of dough hitting hot grease. Patti Page was belting out a tune on the old Philco over the register.

"I'm not keeping you, I hope?" She glanced at his empty plate.

"I'm not in any rush." In his chinos and two-tone shirt rolled up over his forearms, he looked relaxed. No one would have guessed he had an entire crew waiting just up the road.

Cora fiddled with a loose strand of hair, tucking it behind her ear. It had been so long since she'd paid attention to how she looked, this new self-consciousness seemed foreign. "I spoke with my husband," she said. "He—"

"I know," Hank interrupted. "I got a call from him last night."

Cora felt a small, quick stab. How could Jack have done such a thing behind her back? "I'm sorry. He didn't tell me."

"Don't worry about it. We'll find something else." Hank stubbed out his cigarette and reached across the table to lightly cup her hand. There was a faint scar on his forehead that disappeared up into his sandy hair like an extra part, and she stored it away for future reference.

Cora felt a need to explain. "I know this is going to sound ridiculous, but you see my husband has this uncle . . ."

But Hank wasn't listening. "Don't be too hard on him, Cora. He's only looking out for you."

"Me?" She drew back in confusion.

He smiled. "What did you think this was about?"

She stared at him, speechless.

Hank leaned forward. "Look, you're a beautiful

woman. I'd probably do the same thing in his place."

Cora shook her head. "You don't know Jack."

"I don't have to," he said.

Cora sat back, struggling to digest this. When her coffee came, she was content to let Hank do most of the talking. Rubbing the scar on his forehead as he spoke, he told her about his time overseas—he'd been stationed in Italy for most of the war—and about coming home to a Hollywood far different from the one he'd left. American movies were opening to broader interpretations, he said. Movies like *The Searchers*, which she hadn't seen, much less known was existentialist. Listening to him, she felt something kindle inside her, too, as he explained its deeper themes, sketching out scenes in the smoky air.

"I'm running off at the mouth," he said at last, mistaking her rapt silence for a lack of interest. He leaned back in his chair. "What about you, Cora? You haven't told me anything about yourself."

"There isn't much to know."

"Okay. What's your favorite movie then?"

It had been so long since she'd been to the movies, she was embarrassed to say. "With three kids, we don't get out much," she confessed.

"How old are they?"

"Eight, six, and four."

He whistled. "That's a handful."

"At times," she said. "But I wouldn't have it any other way."

"You wouldn't last long in Hollywood with radical ideas like that."

She smiled. "I gather you don't have children of your own."

"Not that I know of." She must have blushed, for Hank instantly sobered. "Sorry, I was just being a smart aleck. The truth is, I'm married to my work. A wife and kids would only end up playing second fiddle."

"You might feel differently someday."

"Let's hope so." He flashed her his rakish grin. "In the meantime, I'll just go on making movies."

She sipped her coffee. "What's this one about?"

"A man who takes a wrong turn on a lonely country road and winds up in heaven. Only not heaven as we imagine it. More like . . . well, like this town." He gestured about him.

"Does he ever find his way back?"

"If I give away the ending you won't go see it," he said with a laugh.

A brief silence fell, and she glanced at her watch to find that half an hour had elapsed. Reluctantly, she rose to her feet. "I should be going. My husband will wonder what's keeping me." She was careful to mention Jack. "Thanks for the coffee. And the stories. I don't feel so bad now about missing our moment of glory."

"Listen, why don't you stop by the set tomorrow?" He rose, too, tossing some bills onto the table. "Bring the kids, if you like. We're filming out on Del Cristo Road. The old schoolhouse. You know it?"

"I ought to. My husband's father and grandfather went to school there. I'm surprised it's still standing." She shook his hand, wishing she could take him up on his offer. "Good-bye, Hank . . . and good luck."

She drifted through the rest of the day feeling oddly out of sync, as if standing at a slight remove watching this cheerful woman who resembled her bustle about, stocking shelves and ringing up purchases. If Jack noticed anything amiss, he didn't remark on it.

Sunday morning she told him she had a headache and wasn't up to mass. It was the first real lie of their marriage. Watching Jack herd the children out the door, she wondered if this was the slippery slope Father Octavio preached about in his sermons, and she was astonished—for Cora had lived her whole life struggling to meet the expectations of others—to realize she didn't care. If this was a sin, she thought, let it be God to whom she answered, not Jack.

She dressed carefully in her best rayon dress, dabbing perfume behind her ears and in the hollow of her throat. Jack had taken the Rambler, leaving only their old Ford pickup, which was used mainly by Guillermo to haul gardening supplies. As she rattled down the hill, she felt more than a little foolish. Would it look as if she were chasing after Hank? A country mouse whose head had been turned by a few idle compliments.

The moment she turned down Del Cristo Lane she forgot her self-consciousness. The old one-room schoolhouse, which had been in use until the new elementary and high schools went up across town just before the war, had been completely transformed. Shiny new panes replaced the boarded-over windows, and a fresh coat of paint brightened the old, peeling clapboard. Even the weeds in front had been mowed, and fresh sod laid in the open area bordered by a tangle of cables, booms, and huge cameras on dollies. In the old schoolyard, tents and trailers formed a ragtag encampment for the small army of actors, extras, and technicians that milled about.

Cora found a place to park, and got out. She spotted Hank by one of the tents, talking to a petite blond woman who looked vaguely familiar. As she drew nearer, Cora recognized her with a mild shock as Selma Lamb, the face on every billboard and magazine cover. She froze in her tracks. But it was too late to turn back. Hank waved, gesturing her over.

"Selma, I want you to meet a friend of mine," he said.

Cora's hand floated up to take Selma's, which felt cool and smooth. A sense of unreality stole over her. Was she really standing here shaking hands with one of the world's biggest stars?

Selma, who looked older in person than on screen, eyed Cora coolly, her lips curving in a little cat smile. "Gotta hand it to you, Hank," she said in a coarse voice that didn't match her face. "You sure do know how to pick 'em. Where'd you find this one?" She gave a low, throaty laugh, and patted Cora's arm. "Relax, honey. It's a compliment."

Cora didn't know what to say. It was as if she

were back in school taking a test she hadn't stud-
ied for. It wasn't just Selma. People swirled
around her, positioning lights and cameras, shout-
ing unintelligible orders. A henna-haired woman
in a blue smock, brushes and combs sprouting
from her pockets, darted over to powder Selma's
nose. Selma paid no more attention to her than
she would a fly.

Hank steered Cora to a canvas chair with his
name in large block letters on the back. "Have a
seat," he said. "We're still setting up, so it'll be a
few minutes."

A man emerged from the one of the tents, a
dead ringer for Burke Howard except he was
shorter, barely over five feet. Then she realized it
was Burke Howard. But how was that possible?
On-screen he looked at least six feet tall.

The henna-haired woman rushed over to powder his nose, fussing with his hair in a way that
seemed . . . well, unmanly. Cora felt embarrassed
for him, though Burke seemed perfectly at ease.
She watched him assume his position on the
schoolhouse steps, marked off with masking tape,
while Selma took hers on the step below—a cinematic sleight of hand that, on-screen, would make
him look as if he were towering over her. They
didn't speak, or even look at each other. They
might have been strangers waiting for a train.
Then the spotlights went on, throwing everything
into sudden, dazzling relief, and Hank boomed,
"Take one! Roll!"

Burke turned to Selma, gazing into her eyes as
if no one else in the world existed.

Selma eyed him just as longingly. "It's not so hard. You say good-bye. Then I say it back." Her voice cracked a little, and her eyes welled with tears. "People have been doing it for thousands of years. What makes us so special?"

Burke brought a hand to her cheek. "I don't know. I'm just an ordinary guy who took a wrong turn on a country road. All I know, Molly, is that if I leave now I'll be walking out on the best thing that's ever happened to me."

"Don't you see? It wasn't meant to be. It's not your time yet. If you stay . . ." She caught her quivering lower lip between her teeth.

He gripped her shoulders, drawing her to him, almost roughly. Selma's head tipped back, honey-blond curls ruffling in the breeze from a giant fan. A microphone dangled from a boom overhead. With his lips grazing hers, Burke choked, "I'd be dead either way you look at it. Whatever happens, wherever I go. I'd be walking around pretending I was alive, but inside I'd be dead. *You hear that, Peter!*" he roared up at the sky.

Selma began to laugh tearily. "You don't have to shout." She pointed toward an elderly white-haired man making his way slowly up the path: Saint Peter in bib overalls clutching a cane in place of a staff.

Just lines from a script, but Cora was caught up in the magic of it. The coarse young woman with the gravelly smoker's voice and her pint-size costar had melted away. She saw only a pair of star-crossed lovers.

Through take after take, she sat mesmerized. It

wasn't until Hank called into his bullhorn, "All right, people, that's a wrap!" that she stirred and shook herself as if from a dream. She watched Hank break away from the huddle of technicians and make his way over to her.

"Not exactly what you were expecting, was it?" he observed, smiling.

"It's a lot harder work than I imagined," she said. "All those takes. How do you know which one to use?"

"I don't . . . until I see it on film. That's the real magic."

"I think I saw a little of that magic just now," she said.

He laughed heartily. "Stick around. It gets old real fast."

"I'd like nothing more, believe me . . . but I really should be going." What would Jack think if he arrived home before her? She rose to her feet. "Thank you. I'll never forget this."

Hank did something that took her completely by surprise. He drew her to him, kissing her lightly on the mouth. A mere brush of lips that was like a bolt of lightning sizzling through her.

The whole way home Cora could feel the imprint of Hank's mouth on hers. She was certain Jack would see it—how could he not?—but when he and the children arrived home minutes after her, he asked only if she was feeling better. She told him no, and he looked disappointed. They'd have to go to Pacific Palisades without her.

Cora was sorry to see them go. She looked forward to weekends with her children. But she couldn't have faced such an outing, not today, with her body on fire with Hank's touch. It would have made a mockery of the outing somehow.

Cora spent the rest of the afternoon moving restlessly from one task to another. It was Lupe's day off, so she had the house to herself. She hemmed a skirt and lined a cupboard. She repotted the African violets on the kitchen windowsill. It was late in the afternoon by the time she sat down to write a long-overdue letter to her father, who seldom bothered to answer the phone. When it was sealed and stamped, she thought, *What now?*

On impulse, Cora reached once more for pen and paper and wrote:

> *Dear Jack,*
> *Feeling better. Decided to take in a movie.*
>
> > *Cora*

She hesitated before adding,

> *P.S. Don't wait up.*

She arrived at the Park Rio in time for the five-thirty showing. The movie, starring Rock Hudson, was sillier than most, but she didn't mind. It was better than sitting home alone. *Written on the Wind* was followed by an equally numbing second feature, the plot of which faded from mind within moments of leaving the theatre.

She climbed into the truck and started the engine. The children would be in bed by now. And

Jack . . . he'd be wondering what was keeping her. All at once, the thought of home beckoned. Yet the old Ford seemed to have a mind of its own. When she reached the intersection of Old Mission and Grove, she found herself turning east instead.

Ten minutes later she was bumping over the narrow dirt lane to Horse Creek Inn. A dude ranch in its heyday in the thirties, it had since fallen on hard times. Its main advantage from Hank's point of view, she supposed, was that there was no shortage of cabins, and no one to look askance at any activities that might've been deemed questionable by people like Ruth Anne. She felt a small shiver of anticipation that bordered on fear.

In the parking area, she got out, picking her way over a footbridge to the main lodge, where a pleasant older woman who was a little hard of hearing told her which cabin was Hank's. "Fourth one on the left. You can't miss it!" she shouted, as if Cora were hard of hearing, too.

Her heart was pounding wildly as she walked between rows of cabins, peering at numbers barely visible in the anemic yellow glow of their porch lights. She heard muffled voices and a radio playing—something jazzy. Her heart pushed up into her throat. What in heaven's name was she doing here? This was insane. *I ought to turn around right now before I make a fool of myself . . . or worse.*

She was on the verge of doing just that when a voice whispered, *He said I was beautiful.* Jack never

told her she was beautiful. All he ever said was,
"You look nice" or "I like you in that dress."

Cora caught her heel on the uneven concrete
path and stumbled. She caught herself and looked
up to find that she was in front of Hank's cabin.
As if in a dream, she floated up the porch steps
and knocked.

From inside came a muffled grunt of displea-
sure, then the faint creak of old floorboards. The
door swung open. Hank stood silhouetted in the
doorway, naked except for a robe that didn't quite
meet in front. Cora quickly averted her eyes, as
stricken as if *she* were the one who'd been caught
half naked. When she looked back at him, the robe
was tied about his waist.

"Cora." He sounded surprised.

"I'm sorry. I've caught you at a bad time." She
took a step back, her face on fire.

"As a matter of fact . . ."

He was interrupted by a soft giggle. Cora glanced
past him into the room, where a naked woman lay
sprawled on the bed amid a tangle of sheets, her
blond head nestled in the crook of one elbow.
Selma. She regarded Cora with cold amusement.
"Don't give it a second thought, sweetie," she called
with a throaty laugh. "You aren't the first, and you
sure as hell won't be the last."

Cora backed away as if from a fire. "I'm sorry.
I . . . I didn't mean . . ." But, of course, she *had*
meant it, hadn't she? For it to be her instead of
Selma.

Hank stepped out onto the porch, catching hold
of her elbow. "Wait." He dropped his voice so

Selma wouldn't hear. "I'm sorry. If you'd called first . . ." His tone made it clear he'd have rearranged his plans.

She shook her head, struggling to hold back tears. "I feel so stupid."

"Don't."

"You must think I'm cheap."

He brought a hand to her cheek, grazing it lightly with his knuckles. Her skin felt bruised where he'd touched her. "I think nothing of the kind," he said gently. "Just the opposite, in fact."

"My husband—"

"There's nothing for him to know." In the yellow glow of the porch light, Hank looked weary all of a sudden—a man who had seen his share of the world and knew enough of its hard ways not to trample on its tender side. When he cupped her chin and leaned forward to brush her mouth with his lips, she sensed his regret. By tomorrow she might be a thing of the past, but at this moment she knew she mattered to him in some small way. "Take care, pretty Cora. Don't forget what you came for."

On the drive home, she puzzled over his words. What had he meant? *Can he possibly imagine I'll find what I'm looking for with Jack?* His idea of an evening out was a town hall meeting or church social. Lovemaking was a hurried, silent affair under the covers at night. Sometimes she thought the Jack who'd written her all those letters was a different man altogether from the one she married.

She arrived home to find him sound asleep on the sofa, a book propped open on his chest. For a long moment she just stood there looking at him, at his face slack with sleep, at the small pink hair barrette—Audrey's—clipped to the pocket of his robe. His nose was sunburned and his wiry hair pushed into a cowlick over one ear. She felt a sudden rush of relief, as if she'd narrowly escaped some calamity.

Jack stirred and blinked up at her. "Cora . . . what is it? What's wrong?"

She touched her cheek and found it wet. She hadn't realized she was crying. "I . . ." She hesitated, not knowing what to say.

It was Jack who rescued her. "Was it the movie?" He yawned and sat up, placing the book on the table by the sofa.

She could barely recall either one. "Oh, you know me. I always cry at happy endings."

Jack gave her an odd look, as if sensing there was something more. She was turning to walk away when he caught her hand, pulling her onto the sofa. Cora dropped her head onto his shoulder with a sigh.

"How was the boardwalk?"

"Fine . . . except we missed you," he said. "I don't think Ray minded about the roller coaster. They all went on the Ferris wheel instead. Sam said it was almost as much fun as watching me lose a dollar on the dime toss." He chuckled softly. "Hey, I almost forgot. How's your headache?"

"All gone," she said.

"That's good." He smiled, brushing a wisp from her forehead.

Cora felt tears well. In the soft glow of the floor

Eileen Goudge

lamp, the room seemed cast in a sepia glow, like an old-time photograph. When she spoke, her voice seemed to come from a distant place she might have been to once, but had forgotten until now existed.

"Jack, do you love me?"

He gave her a startled look. "Of course I do."

"Then say it."

"Cora, what's all this about?"

"I need to hear it."

"What are you talking about? I must have told you a thousand times."

"No . . . you haven't."

"Well, I shouldn't have to. You know how I feel." A familiar look of stubbornness was setting in.

"Do I?" Anger rose in her. "Then why is it we never talk about anything but the kids and the store and what's in today's paper? Why don't you ever tell me I'm pretty? Or that . . . that you want to make love to me?"

Jack's cheeks reddened. "For God's sake, Cora. What's gotten into you?" She caught a note of fear in his voice.

"What's gotten into me," she said, taking a deep breath, "is that half the time I hardly know I'm alive. If it weren't for the children . . ." She caught herself. Until this very moment, she'd never considered divorcing Jack.

The color drained from his cheeks and he slumped back. "You really have no idea, do you?"

She eyed him levelly. "I'm not a mind reader, Jack."

He looked down at his hands, loosely cupped on

his knees, as if the words he wanted to convey had slipped through his fingers somehow. At last, he cleared his throat. "I don't know where to begin."

"How about the night we met?"

He shook his head slowly, lost in memory. "I'd never seen anyone as beautiful. When you said you'd write to me, I thought I'd died and gone to heaven." The words came haltingly, like water from a long-rusted tap. "Only I was afraid if you knew how . . . how strongly I felt, it would scare you off. I guess there's a part of me that still feels that way. I know it doesn't make much sense. The truth is . . ." He raised his eyes to her, and she was shocked to see tears. "You could have had anyone, Cora. I guess part of me is always going to wonder why you chose me."

Cora felt something inside her give way. She touched his cheek. "Oh, Jack, I wish you'd told me. All these years lying next to you, night after night . . ." She caught her lower lip between her teeth.

He looked ashamed. "I guess I haven't been much of a husband."

"It's not all your fault. I didn't know how to ask for what I needed."

"You were my first." He gave a harsh, self-effacing laugh. "I didn't know any more than you on our wedding night."

She was stunned. Jack had led her to believe he'd had plenty of experience before they met. "Why didn't you tell me?"

"I didn't want you to think less of me."

"How could you think that?"

"I don't know. I guess I wasn't thinking straight."
His mouth twisted in a wry smile.

She smiled, too. "It's funny, us talking about this
with three children asleep down the hall."

"We can't turn the clock back," Jack said.

"No, but we can go from here. We can do that,
can't we?"

She brought his hand to her chest, holding it
pressed to her heart. After a moment, when the
stillness grew unbearable, he nudged open the top
button of her blouse. She felt the shy glide of his
palm against her skin and stiffened slightly, her
breath catching in her throat. What if one of the
children walked in?

The same thought must have occurred to Jack,
for he abruptly withdrew his hand. Then Cora
found herself crying in a small, cracked voice,
"Don't stop." For she sensed that if they were to
turn back now, even for as long as it took to climb
the stairs, the spell would be broken. He regarded
her uncertainly, to which she replied, "They'll be
dead to the world."

She unbuttoned her blouse the rest of the way,
turning to let him unhook her bra. His hands were
thick and clumsy, like on their wedding night, and
Cora felt awkward as well. How could she show
him what she wanted when she didn't know
herself?

Yet with each article of clothing shed, she grew
bolder. Stepping out of her slip, she looked down
at Jack on the old plush sofa, where she was certain nothing racier than a good night kiss had ever
taken place. She took in his broad chest with its

triangle of dark hair that disappeared into the creases of his belly. When he opened his arms to her, she sank into them gratefully. In the soft lamplight the husband and wife, who'd always undressed in private and coupled silently under the covers in the dark, explored each another as if for the first time with the shy eagerness of new lovers.

When he slipped a hand between her legs, she whispered, "That feels good," and reached to stroke him in the same way.

She marveled at the softness of his hair, and at the marvelous shape of what she'd known only by thrust. She ran the tips of her fingers over every forbidden nook. The thought of Hank Montgomery surfaced, but only briefly. How could she not have seen this before, how good it could be? Why had it almost taken an affair to make love, *proper* love, to her husband?

When at last he lowered her onto her back and slipped into her, she gasped at the sheer pleasure—pleasure she'd known only in brief flutters before. Was this the same man to whom she'd only dutifully opened her legs these past twelve years? It all seemed so new and wonderful . . . and at the same time like something falling into place. When she looked up into Jack's face, she saw that he felt the same way. His dark eyes were filled with a wild urgency she couldn't have imagined and yes, quite possibly might have run from all those years ago.

The pleasure mounted, gathering to an exquisite point. She moaned, digging her fingers into his back, quivering in every part of her. Then a flood of tingling warmth rushed through her. She bit his shoulder to keep from crying out. Oh, so this was what it was supposed to be like. What she'd ached for without knowing it. Jack's strokes quickened, and then he was climaxing, too.

Afterward, she began to laugh breathlessly.

Mistaking it for something else, he asked anxioulsy, "Was it all right?"

"Oh, Jack. You still don't get it, do you?" She struggled upright.

"Get what?"

"I love you. I've *always* loved you."

He relaxed visibly, drawing her back onto his chest. "I hope you never change your mind." His voice was a deep rumble against her ear.

"Somehow," she said, "I don't think I will."

And she didn't. In the years that followed the spark that had sputtered to life that night was fanned and nurtured. Years later, when a bronze plaque was erected on Sleeping Indian Creek in commemoration of the movie that had brought minor fame to their valley, Cora viewed it as a symbol of sorts. A tangible signpost of the crossroads at which she'd once stood, nearly choosing a path that would have altered the course of her life . . . but in the end saved it. Occasionally, when she and Jack went for a drive after supper, it took them up to the overlook, where they'd stand head to shoulder, arms wrapped loosely about each other's waists, watching the sunset until the last of the pink light had faded.

In 1989, Jack was left partially paralyzed by a

stroke, and Cora rarely left his side. Careful of his pride, she saw to his every need while making it look as if he were doing most of it himself, bathing and dressing him, guiding his hand so he could feed himself. In the morning she read to him from the newspaper—he liked knowing what was going on in the world, if stocks were falling or the price of feed had gone up—and in the evening, popular novels and old favorites like *A Tale of Two Cities*. After a second stroke left him comatose, she was forced to put him in a nursing home. It nearly broke her heart, though every day she remained at his bedside for hour after hour, talking to him as if he could hear her and reading to him like before, except for the occasional tear that slipped out from under the reading glasses she now wore.

Two years later she buried Jack beside his parents on Pilgrim's Mount. Cora was surrounded by her son and daughters, their spouses, and all six of her grandchildren. Later, they all commented on how well she was handling it, and it was true in a way. Her routine seldom varied: gardening in the morning, a brisk walk in the afternoon, dinner with Sam or Audrey, or her old friend Mavis Fitzgerald, whose husband had passed on some years earlier. But privately she grieved, sometimes lurching awake with a cry in the middle of the night, filled with a longing so fierce it seemed worse than death itself. That was when she envied Jack for being the first to go, when she hated him for not taking her, too.

In Cora's seventy-fifth year, Irma Littleton's

grandson, to whom she'd left the Park Rio when she died, had the bright idea of hosting a film festival. He even found a big name director to host it, which had the effect of drawing young filmmakers hoping to be discovered. There were even a few museum pieces, like eighty-year-old Hank Montgomery, largely forgotten now except by students of film history.

Cora, who attended the cocktail reception, scarcely recognized him. Hank had lost most of his hair, and in his once handsome face she saw the magnificent ruin of a life lived full throttle, damn the consequences. She approached him tentatively, not sure if he would remember her.

"Mr. Montgomery? I'm Cora Delarosa. I used to own the general store." It was Sam's now. Cora had given it to her when she sold Isla Verde to Sam and Martin a few years back.

His eyes clouded over—he seemed to be struggling to place her—and then recognition dawned. "Well, I'll be damned. Sure, I remember." He grinned, and something young and vital surfaced in his old-man's face. "Look at you. As pretty as ever."

She touched her hair, which was silver now. "I'm not so sure I agree with you," she said with a smile, "but I appreciate the compliment."

He clasped her hand in his large, spotted one, holding on for so long Cora began to wonder uneasily if he was ever going to let go. "Your husband?"

"He passed away two years ago," she told him. "I'm sorry to hear that." Hank let go of her hand, the spark going out of his eyes as he did. He seemed to be ruminating on events in his own life.

She cocked her head, putting on a look of bright interest. "What about you? Didn't I read that you got married?"

"Several times, as a matter of fact." He chuckled, a hoarse rasp that sent him into a coughing fit. His face reddened, and just when she began to grow alarmed he straightened and croaked, "Damn cigarettes. Should've given them up years ago."

"It's not too late," she said.

He shot her a keen look. His eyes were the same vivid blue she recalled from all those years ago. "That's what my doctor keeps telling me. I don't believe a word of it. It's all behind us, isn't it? Everything we thought was so important."

She lifted her glass. "Well, here's to past successes then."

"May they live long in memory." He clinked his glass to hers.

She glanced over his shoulder and saw a bearded young director headed their way, clearly on a mission. "I should let you go," she said. "I'm sure there are dozens of people who want to talk to you. I just wanted to say hello."

She was turning to go when she felt his hand on her arm, heavy and somehow insistent. "Wait," he said. "I remember you were looking for something. Did you ever find it?"

Cora turned slowly to face him, wearing a look of such shining sweetness that those who happened to glance her way were transfixed. In that moment she was every hope ever realized; she was what dreamers dream and lovers seek. She was a lifetime of memories distilled into a heartbeat.

"Oh, yes," she said. "I most certainly did."

From
STRANGER IN
PARADISE

BOOK ONE OF THE CARSON SPRINGS TRILOGY

Available in paperback from Signet
in June 2002

"Sam." A familiar voice, low and musical.

She turned around, startled to find Ian standing before her. How had he managed to sneak in without her noticing? Heat rushed up into her cheeks, and she darted a furtive glance over her shoulder. No one was looking their way. "What are you doing here?" she whispered.

He flashed her an easy grin. "I didn't realize I needed an invitation."

"You know what I mean."

He didn't appear the least bit fazed. In the same unhurried voice, he asked, "Is there somewhere we can talk? In private?"

She cast another glance over her shoulder. Laura was waiting on someone, and only one other customer was wandering about. "All right," she said, "but only for a minute."

She led the way to the tiny office in back, just large enough for a desk and file cabinet. There was no point offering him a seat. She nudged the door shut with her heel. The pounding of her heart seemed to fill the tiny, windowless space.

She didn't wait for him to speak. "Ian, listen, yesterday was . . . unbelievable. I don't regret it for a moment. But it can't go any further." She closed her eyes, leaning against the file cabinet. The metal felt cool against her burning skin.

"Because of the age thing?" He sounded more puzzled than anything.

"It's complicated."

"It doesn't have to be."

"For you."

"For either of us."

He stepped toward her, and suddenly she was in his arms. Oh God. How easy it was, like sliding into a warm bath. As if her mind had become separated from her body somehow. A body with a will of its own. She felt his mouth on hers, his sly tongue. . . .

Just this once, she pleaded, as if to some higher authority. After that, no more. If she was to have any chance of resisting him in the days to come she'd have to end it. Here. Now.

The question was, *How?*

Wrapped in Ian's arms, lost in a kiss with no beginning and therefore no end, Sam wasn't aware of the door easing open behind her.

"Oh God, I'm sorry. I didn't realize."

Sam broke away from Ian. Her daughter stood in the doorway, gaping as if at a car wreck. Cheeks flushed and eyes wide with horror, a corner of her mouth flickering in an interrupted smile. Then, with a tiny cry, Laura scurried off.

Alice was showered and dressed before Wes was even up, yesterday's conversation with her sister still echoing in her head. To think this had been going on the whole time she'd been on her honeymoon, and she was only just hearing about it. Couldn't Laura have dropped her a line?

Breakfast was a slice of buttered toast washed down with black coffee strong enough to jumpstart a battery. Then she was out the door, leaving her husband to weed through three weeks' worth of mail. She hadn't driven more than a hundred yards when she fished her cell phone from her purse and punched in Laura's number.

"It's me. I'm on my way over." The top was down on her Porsche Carrera, a gift from Wes, and she had to raise her voice to be heard.

"I'll make another pot of coffee." Laura sounded anything but glum. Alice heard the sound of running water and faint judder of old pipes. "You had breakfast yet?"

"I'm not coming over to eat."

"Let me guess? You're on your way to Mom's."

"Not me. *Us*."

"Count me out." Her sister groaned. "I'm up to my ears in . . . you don't even want to know."

"Hey, you're the one who called me, remember?"

Laura sighed. "I know, but I've thought about it—I was up most of last night, as a matter of fact—and I'm not sure it's our place to be telling her how to run her life."

"We're not *telling* her anything," Alice said. "Just reminding her of what's at stake here."

There was a pause. In the background, she could hear a blend of voices, one deep and masculine—that would be Hector's—the other soft and tentative. Then Laura said, "I'm sure Mom's given it a lot of thought, too. She's not exactly the impulsive type."

"*Wasn't*. We're talking past tense here."

"Okay, but suppose she isn't interested in hearing what we have to say? What then?"

"She owes it to Dad to at least listen."

"What's Dad got to do with it?"

"How's it going to look?" Alice went on as if she hadn't spoken. "Mom gallivanting around town with her lover to all the places Dad and she . . ." She bit down on her lower lip, feeling as if she were going to cry.

"Oh, Al. I feel terrible. I shouldn't have made such a big deal of it." Laura was beating herself up again. Why did she always think everything was her fault? "Look, maybe it'll all blow over in a week or two."

There was a surge of static and Laura's voice faded. "We'll talk about it when I get there!" Alice yelled. She thumbed the END button and flipped the phone shut.

The sky was a cloudless sprawl overhead, the warm wind rushing at her a reminder of Kapalua, with its frangipani-scented breeze and mimosa sunsets . . . and the certainty she'd felt about Wes. Her hands tightened about the wheel. *Was* she making too big a deal of this? In the world of television, people had affairs all the time. Older men with younger women; older women with younger men. No one had batted so much as an eyelash when Lainie Bacheler—widow of CBS mogul Marvin Bacheler, who admitted to being sixty, which meant she was older—showed up at last year's Emmys on the arm of a man young enough to be her grandson.

But this wasn't L.A., and her mother was anything but the usual fodder for wagging tongues. And oh, how they would wag!

The poor dear, I had no idea she was so desperate.

It's obvious what this is about. What else could she want from a man young enough to be her son?

Martin will be rolling over in his grave.

Alice made the turn onto Grove, distracted at that moment by the tumbledown building on her right—the town's original one-room schoolhouse, where both her great-grandfather and grandfather had gone to school. Its windows were boarded over and its paint coming away in curly strips; litter lay in a small drift against the padlocked door. In her day it had been a prime high school make-out spot. Her boyfriend, Bif Holloway, used to park under that tree over there, where they'd kiss until her mouth was raw. But it had another distinction as well: in the Fifties a scene in *Stranger in Paradise,* referred to locally as The Movie, was filmed there.

Alice's favorite story of her grandmother's was of the time she'd sneaked off to visit the set one Sunday while the rest of the family was at church. The biggest surprise, she'd said, was that the stars who'd looked ten feet tall on screen were short—practically midgets. It wasn't like watching a play,

either. There'd been take after take, with a lumpy
woman in a cardigan scurrying over with a hair-
brush and hairspray between each one. Not very
glamorous, to be sure, though her grandmother
always grew misty-eyed when speaking of its director, Hank Montgomery. "Handsomest man I
ever saw," she'd sigh. "Oh, he was quite the ladies' man!" It was Alice's first peek—if only vicar-
iously—behind the plush curtain, and the lure of
show business had been with her ever since.

Her sister's house was in full swing when she
arrived, the kitchen a jumble of boots, jackets
slung over the backs of chairs, dogs and cats nos-
ing at bowls of kibble lined up along the base-
board. There was Hector, hunched over his plate
at the table, and Maude at the sink washing up.
Laura stood at the counter, a mug of coffee in one
hand and a tattered recipe card in the other.

"I can't remember if Grandma's banana cake
calls for one cup of flour or two. That part is
smudged." She peered at the card. "Or maybe I
need reading glasses."

"Don't ask me. I wouldn't have a clue." Alice
nodded hello to Hector. "Hey, Hec. Missed you
at the wedding."

She tried not to sound offended. It wasn't per-
sonal, she knew. As long as she'd known him,
Hector had been this way: a genial loner. With
one exception—he'd always taken his meals with
the family. Her mother had insisted on it, and
from the start he'd put up little resistance. Not
until years later, after a number of his brothers
and sisters had migrated north as well, did she

realize how hard it had to have been, leaving his own family behind. Proof lay in the fact that Hector remembered each and every one of his twenty-two nieces' and nephews' birthdays, even the ones he'd never met. His room in back of the barn was a gallery of family photos tilting from pushpins.

He flashed her a disarming smile, revealing the tooth chipped in a fistfight back in his rowdier days. "Heard all about it from your sister." There wasn't a hint of apology in his voice. "Me? I'm holding out for the pictures."

"It was such a beautiful wedding." Maude turned from the sink, beaming at Alice as she wiped her soapy hands on her apron. "And such a beautiful bride."

"You were quite the belle of the ball yourself." Alice recalled Maude's unusual, but oddly fashionable getup. "By the way, Maude, thanks for the . . . um . . ." What *had* she given them? "The letter organizer. I'm sure it'll come in handy."

The old woman smiled sweetly. "Actually, dear, it's a toast caddy."

Alice winced at her blunder. On the other hand, who in this century, on this side of the Atlantic, would give someone a silver-plated toast caddy? "Well," she said brightly, "since we usually eat breakfast on the run we'll get more use out of it this way."

"That's how she stays so thin," Laura groused good-naturedly. With a sigh she tucked the recipe card back into its box. "I give up. I'll make devil's food instead."

"What's the occasion?" Alice asked.

"Finch," she said. "It's her birthday. Would you believe she's never had a birthday cake, not even the store-bought kind? What kind of parents would—" The thump of boots on the porch caused her to break off. Pearl and Rocky dashed to the door, barking excitedly.

It was the girl. "I cleaned out the stalls like you asked, and—" She caught sight of Alice, halting abruptly. "Hi." Her eyes were dark glints behind the screen door's buckled mesh. Then with a look of resolve she pushed it open and stepped inside.

Alice hardly recognized her. In just three weeks she'd filled out; in an old pair of jeans and clean white T-shirt she looked like any teenager. Her dark hair was pulled back in a ponytail, and she'd lost that awful haunted look. "Happy birthday, Finch." Alice struck a casual tone. "I hope you plan to celebrate by doing something a little more exciting than mucking out stalls."

The girl's cheeks reddened, and she dropped her gaze.

Laura quickly stepped in. "I thought we'd take a ride later on," she said. "You haven't seen anything until you've seen the view from the hill."

Finch shrugged. "Sure, whatever."

"The poppies are in bloom. You won't believe how beautiful they are." She turned to Alice brightly, as if she hadn't noticed how Finch had withdrawn. "I've been giving her lessons. Wait till you see her—she's a natural."

Some of the stiffness went out of the girl's

shoulders. She flashed Laura a look that seemed to say, *I know you mean well, but I'm not ready to trust you.* "I'd better go take a shower," she muttered, sidling past them.

Alice waited until she heard the thud of the door down the hall. "Any word on her parents?"

"Not a peep." Maude sighed, tucking a wisp of ivory hair into her bun. She might have been Auntie Em fretting over Dorothy. "Poor child. To think what she must have gone through . . ."

"I'm not pushing it for now." Laura spoke with unaccustomed firmness. "She'll come around when she's ready. Meanwhile, she's welcome to stay as long as she likes."

Alice wondered if her sister was getting in over her head. "Don't let it drag out too long. She has a home . . . somewhere. I'm sure her parents will want to know where she is."

Hector rose and carried his plate over to the sink. "Excuse me, ladies, but I have work to do." The abruptness of his tone spoke louder than any words; he might just as well have told Alice to mind her own business.

She tried not to feel hurt. Hector, though polite and friendly to everyone, had always been closest to Laura—maybe because he thought she needed someone to stick up for her. It was a special bond that went both ways. Even now, Alice couldn't help noticing the way her sister's gaze followed Hector onto the porch, where he retrieved his hat from a rusty nail and slapped it against his thigh. For several long seconds after he stepped down into the yard, Laura's eyes remained fixed on the motes of dust swirling lazily in the shaft of sunlight where he'd stood.

She's in love with him, Alice thought. She recalled Laura's long-ago crush that only a blind man could have missed. Hector wasn't blind, just discreet. Laura had been just a teenager, after all, even if he hadn't been much older. Then there was Peter. She wondered if Hector would be so discreet now.

Alice was distracted by the newspaper on the table. A headline jumped out at her: SLAIN MAN'S IDENTITY REMAINS UNKNOWN. She scanned the article. Something about a transient found stabbed to death in the hills above Horse Creek. How ghastly. The last murder she could recall was that old booze hound, Anson Grundig, battering his poor wife to death, but that had to have been eight or nine years ago. Carson Springs wasn't exactly a hotbed of crime.

"What do you know about this?" she asked.

"It happened last Friday," Laura said. "No suspects yet, as far as I know. The police are still looking."

"I can hardly sleep nights just thinking of it." Maude's soft little cushion of a face seemed to fold in on itself. "A stranger on the loose, out to murder innocent people."

"It could be someone we know," Alice said.

Maude grew visibly pale.

Laura shot Alice a warning look, saying pointedly, "Don't you have to be somewhere?"

Alice glanced at her watch. "You're right. We should be going."

Laura looked about to protest, then sighed, forking a hand through hair already scrambled. "Okay, okay. Just give me a minute to throw something on." She glanced down at her rumpled shorts and T-shirt as if just now noticing what she was wearing. "God knows what Mom would do without us to keep her in line, right?"

In the car, traveling east along Old Sorrento Road past houses much like Laura's—most with barns and the requisite horse trailer out front—it occurred to Alice that she had no idea how serious this was. What if it was more than just sex? What if they were actually *in love*? She couldn't picture her mother moving in with Ian. That would leave only one other option: Ian would have to move into Isla Verde.

He'd be sleeping in the bed she shared with Dad. Sitting in his place at the table . . .

Alice felt slightly sick.

The road began to slope downward as they neared Sorrento Creek. They rattled over a cattle grid, past a sunny pasture dotted with oaks and sycamores, in which cows grazed peacefully. Rising over the next hill were the vine-shrouded walls of Our Lady of the Wayside.

Alice recalled the time she and her sister had sneaked into the convent. She'd been ten and Laura twelve. All they knew of the nuns' sequestered existence was what their mother's friend, Gerry, had told them. Nothing could have pre-

pared them for what lay behind those forbidden
walls: the lush garden and quaint storybook buildings, the chapel from which sweet voices floated
like a chorus of angels. It was just after dawn—
they'd slipped away while their parents were
asleep, riding their bicycles two miles in the near
dark—and they were ravenous. Alice was reach-
ing to pluck an orange from a tree when a voice
rang out.

"Don't touch that."

A tall, stern-faced nun strode from the shadows
of the chapel, a prayer book in one hand and ro-
sary beads in the other. She cast a long blade of
shadow in the rising sun.

"We . . . we were just looking," Alice managed
to squeak.

"Where are your parents?"

"They don't know we're here." Laura, white
with terror, stepped in front of Alice as if to pro-
tect her.

"I see." The tall nun appeared to be pondering
what sort of punishment they should receive.
"Come with me." She turned and began making
her way down the path.

They'd had no choice but to follow her,
trembling all the way, down a winding path and
up a short flight of steps. After what seemed an
eternity they reached a building covered in vines,
like the chapel, with a cross carved in the stone
arch above its stout wooden door and a statue of
the Virgin Mary in front.

Inside it was cool and dark and smelled like
church. They walked down a long corridor, their

reflections shimmering ghostlike on the waxed tiles, into a large, open-beamed kitchen filled with light. A wooden table stretched along one wall. The nun sat them down, giving them each a bowl of oatmeal from the pot on the stove.

"I'm Mother Ignatius," she said, not unkindly. She set out milk and honey. Alice saw that she was old—older than their parents—her face wreathed in lines, her blue eyes nested in crinkles. "When you're finished with your breakfast, I'll take you home."

Alice shot her a startled look. "How?" Nuns, to the best of her knowledge, had no means of transportation.

Mother Ignatius frowned in puzzlement; then the creases in her forehead smoothed. "Oh, the usual way. On angels' wings."

Alice wished they were on angels' wings now. For she had the uneasy feeling this mission— much as it might be for their mother's own good—was anything but merciful. Wes's words came back to her. *Your mother's only human. . . .*

She thought again of her father. How could she sit still while her mother made a fool of herself? While she dragged Dad's memory through the mud? Long after Ian was gone, the taint would remain. Alice frowned and pressed down a little harder on the gas pedal.

They turned south onto Chumash, where pastures gave way to citrus and avocado groves. Through the trees Alice caught a glimpse of a ramshackle farmhouse—the old Truesdale place. No one had seen Dick Truesdale since his wife's death more than five years ago. It was rumored he'd taken to his bed and was now almost an invalid.

Minutes later they were pulling to a stop in front of their mother's house—the house Alice would always think of as her grandparents'. As she climbed from the car a familiar sound greeted her: the swishing of Lupe's broom. Alice could see her mother's elderly housekeeper through the wrought iron gates to the courtyard: a rawhide strip of a woman attacking its tiles with her broom as if beating a snake to death.

"Lupe! For heaven's sake come in out of that heat," called an exasperated voice from inside.

Alice and Laura exchanged a glance. Their mother had been nagging Lupe to slow down as long as they could remember. Nothing ever changed—which, in light of their own task, provided little comfort. Laura lingered in the driveway.

"Are you sure we should go through with this?"

"We don't have a choice," Alice said.

"Remember those embarrassing talks about the birds and the bees?" Her sister groaned. "Who'd have thought we'd one day be having the same conversation with *her*?"

They made their way up the path. The pergola, ablaze in climbing black-eyed Susan, was a cool tunnel after the hot drive. A wind chime tinkled softly amid the stubborn swishing of Lupe's broom.

Lupe didn't see them at first, so intent was she on her task. Leaves from the potted citrus trees had been swept into neat little piles. A dustpan heaped with bougainvillea blossoms sat on the edge of the lily pond. Then she looked up, her wrinkled brown face breaking into a delighted grin.

"*Ay, mis hijitas*. No one told me you were coming."

"It was sort of spur of the moment." Laura glanced uneasily at Alice.

Lupe propped her broom against a pillar and walked over to hug them.

She playfully pinched Alice's waist. "Marriage must agree with you. You've put on a few pounds." Her brown eyes sparkled. "Unless it's a baby on the way."

Heat rose in Alice's cheeks. *You'd better get used to it. You'll be hearing it for the next ten or fifteen years.* But something kept her from telling Lupe she had no intention of ever having a baby. Never mind Lupe. How would her family take it? Her poor sister, for whom motherhood wasn't an option. And her mother, who'd be devastated to learn there'd be no grandchildren.

"More like too many piña coladas." Alice managed a weak laugh.

"*Lupe . . .*" Sam called once more.

The old woman sighed as if to say, *You see what I have to put up with?* Shaking her head and muttering something unintelligible under her breath, she retrieved her broom and went on sweeping.

Just as they so often had in childhood, the two sisters wordlessly joined hands, stepping up onto the low porch and letting themselves in the door.

The house was little changed from their grandparents' day. Worn Navajo rugs were scattered over the terra-cotta tiled floor, and in the sunny, white-walled living room the Mission oak furniture stood out in stark relief. The only real difference was the bright Mexican folk art that had replaced the gloomy old paintings of the previous era.

Sam must have heard them, for she appeared just then, wearing a look of pleasant surprise. "Alice! When did you get back? You should have called to let me know you were coming."

Alice eyed her in disbelief. Could this be their mother? Sam's auburn hair was pulled back in a ponytail that revealed a pair of dangly, silver-and-turquoise earrings. Her cheeks were aglow and her gray-green eyes sparkled. Even the outfit she was wearing was new—a silky teal top and matching trousers that rippled like water about her slender frame.

A knot formed in Alice's stomach. *A woman only looks that way when she's in love.* Clearly, they had their work cut out for them.

from
TASTE OF HONEY

BOOK TWO OF THE CARSON SPRINGS TRILOGY

Available in hardcover from Viking
in June 2002

Gerry cupped her hands around her mouth, calling, "Sam! Ian!"

No answer.

Please, God, don't let them be dead. She thought of the baby due in just two weeks. It wasn't fair. Not after everything they'd been through. They had to be okay, they *had* to be.

She lost her footing and skidded the rest of the way down, catching hold of a low-hanging branch just in time to keep from tumbling over the sharp drop-off into the stream. She landed on her backside with a jolt a few dozen feet from Sam's Honda.

She hauled herself upright, shrieking, *"Sam!"*

The car lay on its side, the door to the driver's side sticking straight up like a hatch and the bushes around it broken and flattened as if someone had crawled out. The only thing keeping it from plunging into the creek below was the stout tree against which it was wedged. Holding herself braced against the steering wheel, she reached down into the shadowy recesses of the front seat. Her fingers danced along a limp arm to grasp hold of Sam's wrist. Its warmth traveled through her like an electrical current, and she went dizzy with relief.

Alive. Oh, thank God.

"Sam? It's me . . . Gerry."

Sam stirred and blinked up at her uncomprehendingly. "Whuuu . . . ?"

"You were in an accident."

Sam's hand jerked free to cradle her belly. "The baby," she croaked.

"The baby's fine. You're fine." Gerry's voice was a high, thin warble. She felt as if she'd drunk ten cups of coffee on an empty stomach. If she could just keep it up, keep talking, keep from losing it. "Does it feel like anything's broken?"

"I . . . I don't think so." Sam's ashen face twisted suddenly, and she pressed down on her belly, saying through gritted teeth, "The baby . . . oh, God . . . I think it's coming."

The world all at once seemed to recede, as if Gerry were looking at it through the wrong end of a telescope, seeing only the twisted rearview mirror peering up at her like a darkly glittering eye, the strap of Sam's purse caught on the gear shift, and Sam's dear face peering up at her from the shadows—a pale cameo in a tarnished setting.

From somewhere deep inside, she mustered the necessary calm. "Andie called for help. You'll be at the hospital before you know it," she soothed, groping until she found the buckle on Sam's seat belt. The click of it releasing might have been a gun going off in the stillness.

Sam gripped her hand. "Where's Ian? Is he all right?"

Gerry pried her fingers loose. "He's a little beat-up, but otherwise fine. Don't worry. You'll both be seeing this baby into the world—a nice, fat healthy baby. This is just a bump in the road, that's all." She smiled grimly at the unintended pun. "Did you think you were going to go about this like any normal person? After the way this baby was conceived? Oh, I know I had you beat hands down in that department—" she thought of Claire, *her* baby, lost in another lifetime, who'd come back to her in a way she couldn't have imagined all those years ago, "but even *I* couldn't have come up with anything this rich. As if having a baby weren't enough, you had to go and turn it into an episode of *ER*."

Sam managed a weak smile. "Does this mean I get to meet George Clooney?"

"Meet him? He'll be standing in line for *your* autograph." Gerry gave a small, teary laugh.

Sam's face contorted, and she once again seized hold of Gerry's hand, gripping it tight enough to cut off circulation. "I feel something *down there*. Oh, Gerry, I . . . I think I'm bleeding."

"Are you sure your water didn't break?" Now she *did* hear panic in her voice.

"P-pretty sure."

"Hang on, kiddo. Any minute now." Where the hell was that ambulance?

Then, blessedly, she heard it.

The sky above, in all its magnificent sprawl, seemed to mock her, the thought of Aubrey swooping down like a falling star: his pregnant wife crushed to death in a car wreck. For the first time she truly understood what it must have been like for him, and why their own affair hadn't stood a chance. Wasn't that the real reason he was on his way to Brussels now?

The thought was driven from her head by the crunch of tires, and headlights panning in an arc overhead. As if from another plane she heard the slam of car doors, followed by the babble of voices—Andie's among them, high and anxious. Light from the ambulance's pulsing dome washed down the slope, tingeing the foliage around her a lurid red, and now she could make out a pair of jumpsuit-clad figures expertly picking their way down the slope, a travois bobbing between them.

She smiled at Sam. "Relax, kiddo. The Marines have landed."

Gerry peered down into Sam's pale, anxious face. A kind of tent had been erected over the operating table on which she lay, shielding her lower half from view. Her hair was tucked under a cap like the one Gerry had on, and Gerry was reminded of when they'd been in high school primping for dates. Right now, Sam might have been a scared sixteen-year-old.

"I wasn't sure you'd get here in time," she said weakly.

Gerry took her hand and squeezed it gently. "What good is an understudy who can't go on when the leading man breaks his leg?"

On the other side of the tent, doctors and nurses flitted in and out of view. A monitor beeped and instruments clattered against a tray. The doctor, quietly issuing orders, might have been speaking Swahili for all Gerry knew, or cared.

"I can't lose this baby," Sam said hoarsely. Her eyes swam with tears.

"Hush, now. What a thing to say," Gerry scolded, only mildly taken aback to hear her mother's voice emerge from her mouth. "You're going to be just fine. The baby, too."

"I know I didn't want it at first." Sam's chin began to tremble, and a tear slipped down her temple. "Do you think God is punishing me?"

"God doesn't punish you for thoughts. It's only actions that count. And there's no mother as good or loving." Gerry started to take a swipe at her own brimming eyes before remembering she was gloved, and drew her arm across them instead. "Dammit. *Now* look what you made me do. And here I was, saving my tears for the christening."

On the other side of the tented sheet, Gerry heard Inez instruct briskly, "Okay . . . we're cutting through the fascia . . . let's have some suction."

Sam gripped her hand. "I don't feel it. I don't feel a *thing*. Just . . . pressure. How do I know if he's okay?"

"I'll bet you ten dollars it's a girl," Gerry replied in the hope of distracting her.

She was rewarded by the faintest whisper of a smile. "You're on."

They fell silent, overcome by the awesomeness of it all. Then Inez announced with reassuring authority, "We're cutting through the amniotic sac now . . . I've got the head . . . okay, now a shoulder." She paused. "Oh, my goodness, it's a boy!"

"A boy." Sam's voice was soft with wonder.

Gerry grinned. "Looks like I'm out ten bucks."

They waited for the familiar sound that would put all their fears to rest, and when it didn't come, Sam stared at the sheet as if she could burn a hole through it. "He's not crying. What's happening? *Is he all right?*"

Gerry was worried, too, but she patted Sam's shoulder. "Relax. Inez knows what she's doing." Though admittedly Andie's and Justin's births had been a Sunday walk in the park compared to this.

Not like your first one.

A memory glimmered in the dim recesses of her mind. Then suddenly, in her mind, she was being whisked down a corridor on a gurney. The pains no longer coming in waves, but gripping her like a giant unseen fist. She cried out that she felt sick, but the nurse at her side merely smiled and said it would all be over soon. She didn't understand that Gerry was telling her she had to throw up. When she *did*, the beady-eyed woman looked annoyed.

"Where's my mother? I want my mother!" Gerry cried with the anguish of a girl barely out of her teens who'd never known sickness without Mavis's bending over her with a cool cloth and a soothing hand.

"Your mother is waiting outside," the nurse informed her. "Now be a good girl, and stop making such a fuss."

When Gerry opened her mouth to curse, an anguished howl emerged instead. The pain had ascended to new heights, not just gripping but *tearing* at her from the inside out.

A set of double doors swung open, and the gurney bumped over a threshold. A man's face, its lower half obscured from view by the mask he had on, loomed into view. All she could see were a pair of bright blue eyes netted in wrinkles and bushy white-blond brows. "How are we doing, Miss Fitzgerald, hmm?" His lips moving beneath the mask made her think of Boris Karloff in *The Mummy*.

"Where's my doctor?" she croaked.

"Doctor DeCordillera is out of town," she was told. "I'm Doctor Perault. I'm filling in for him."

Gerry shook her head. No, she didn't want some stranger. She started to protest, but no one seemed to care what she wanted. She was lifted onto a table and her feet placed in stirrups. Something cold was swabbed over her privates, which in the past twelve hours had come to seem like public property instead—poked and prodded and shaved, and now mercilessly on view.

It soon ceased to matter, though, for the area between her legs might have been the burning gates of hell. She writhed and screamed and begged, but no one took pity. That's when she knew for certain that God was punishing her, that she was only getting what she deserved.

"Push." The command was muffled by the roaring in her ears. "Give us a big push now. Good. Now one more. You're doing fine. Take a deep breath. Okay, again. *Push!*"

"I can't!" she screamed, feeling as if she were being split right down the middle. She pictured a ripe avocado from which the baby would be scooped like a pit.

But somehow she *was* pushing. Grunting and heaving like an animal all the while. A minute later something warm squirted out between her legs. The pain abruptly eased, and she fell back gasping. She could hear a baby crying, but sweat was pouring down her forehead into her eyes and she couldn't see it—only a blur of flailing limbs, a thatch of whorled hair.

"A girl!" she heard a nurse crow.

She held out her arms. "Let me hold her."

A swaddled bundle was placed on her chest, a pair of blue eyes peering intently up at her from its folds. A great love welled up inside her, and she instantly forgot the torment of a moment ago. She watched the little rosebud mouth purse as if in anticipation of being fed, and felt an answering tingle in her breasts.

Abruptly, the baby was lifted from her arms.

"It's better this way, dear," the nurse told her. In her mask and gown, she might have been a thief robbing Gerry of all she held dear.

"No . . . wait." Gerry wanted to cry out that

she'd changed her mind. How could she have known what she'd be giving up when she'd signed those papers? But it was too late; the nurse, along with her baby, was gone.

EILEEN'S RECIPES

Heavenly Triple-Decker Delight Brownies

This was sent to me by Jolene Hampton White of Anderson Township, Ohio. I made them over Christmas and they got rave reviews. They're easy to make, too, with results that are a chocoholic's dream.

Bottom Layer:

½ cup butter
4 oz. unsweetened
  chocolate
1½ cups sugar
3 eggs
1½ tsp. vanilla extract

1 tsp. espresso powder
  mixed with 1 tsp.
  boiling water
1 cup flour
½ tsp. salt

Heat oven to 350 degrees, and grease a 9-inch square baking pan. Place butter and chocolate in a microwave-safe bowl. Microwave for 1 minute, stir, and microwave for 1 minute more. Stir smooth. In a separate bowl, beat together sugar and eggs. Stir in the chocolate, vanilla extract, and espresso sludge. Add flour and salt, and stir until thoroughly blended. Pour into greased pan. Bake for 20 to 25 minutes, or until toothpick inserted in middle comes out clean. (Don't overbake!) Let sit until cool, at least one hour.

Filling:

¼ cup softened butter   1½ to 3 Tbsps. milk
2½ cups confectioner's   ½ tsp. almond extract
  sugar

Cream the butter and confectioner's sugar. Add the milk 1 Tbsp. at a time, beating until filling is smooth and spreadable. Beat in almond extract. Frost the cooled brownies, cover, and chill for 1 hour. (Note: For Christmas, you can tint the frosting with red or green food coloring for a festive touch).

Topping:

¾ cup semisweet choco-   3 Tbsps. butter
  late chips

Pour chips into a microwave-safe bowl. Add butter, and microwave for 1½ minutes or until chocolate melts. Stir smooth. Pour melted chocolate over chilled brownies and quickly smooth to an even thickness with knife. Refrigerate for 45 minutes or until the coating hardens. Let the brownies come to room temperature before cutting. Use sharp knife dipped in hot water, then wiped dry, to make nice, clean cuts.

Makes 2 to 2½ dozen brownies, depending on size.

Piña Colada Cake

Another crowd pleaser. It's fun, festive, and just tropical enough to make you think of an island beach, palms swaying overhead, and a cool drink in hand. It's also a perfect compliment to hot tea on those chilly days when you'd prefer to stay indoors.

1¼ cups (2½ sticks) butter, at room temperature

1¾ cups granulated sugar

5 eggs, at room temperature

1 teaspoon almond or rum extract

¾ cup milk

2¼ cups unbleached white flour

⅓ cup cornstarch

1½ cups unsweetened grated coconut (available in health food stores; if substituting sweetened variety, whir in food processor or blender to chop and reduce granulated sugar to 1½ cups)

1 tsp. baking powder

½ tsp. baking soda

1 jar maraschino cherries

1 8-oz. can pineapple chunks in own juice

confectioner's sugar

Preheat oven to 325 degrees (275 degrees for convection ovens). Butter and flour a 9-inch bundt or tube pan. Cream butter and sugar with electric mixer until light in color, (about five minutes). Add eggs one at a time. When thoroughly blended, add almond or rum extract, and milk.

Meanwhile, drain cherries and pineapple chunks in a colander over sink or bowl. With small sharp knife, cut cherries into halves or thirds. Cut pineapple chunks into thirds (you can use crushed pineapple, if well drained, but the consistency will be slightly different).

In separate bowl, mix together flour, cornstarch, coconut, baking powder, and baking soda. Add to butter-egg mixture all at once, mixing well. Stir in chopped cherries and pineapple until evenly blended. Spoon batter into pan. Use back of spoon to push batter higher up along the outer edges of the pan (this helps to prevent it from puffing up in the center while baking).

Bake for 1 hour, or until a toothpick inserted in the center comes out clean (don't overbake!) Let cool for 20 minutes. Loosen edges with a small knife. Unmold cake onto a plate. Let cool to room temperature. Dust with confectioner's sugar before serving.

Yields 16 slices.

GARDEN OF LIES
0-451-16291-9/$7.99

Rachel and Rose grew up worlds apart—
Rachel in the lap of Manhattan luxury, Rose
in the New York slums. But neither of
them knows the tie between them—
a terrible secret that began with birth
and that will draw them ever closer
as both fall in love with the same man—
until they are face-to-face with the
truth about each other and themselves.
"Pretty terrific . . . satisfying . . . heart
lifting." —*Chicago Tribune*

SUCH DEVOTED SISTERS
0-451-17337-6/$7.50

Sisters Annie—proprietess of a
glamorous and famous Madison Avenue
chocolate shop—and Laurel—a quiet but
sought-after illustrator—vie for the
heart of the same man, who loves them
both. Sweeping from Paris to the
Caribbean, this is the searing story of a
blood bond, family secrets and
betrayals, and a passion that forces two
sisters to make difficult decisions.
"Double-dipped passion . . .
Irresistible." —*San Francisco Chronicle*

BLESSING IN DISGUISE
0-451-18404-1 / $7.50

Grace, the white daughter of a powerful
senator, enjoys a life of genteel
affluence in Georgia, while Nola, a
young black woman determined to
succeed as an architect, struggles with
near-poverty in Washington, D.C.
Yet the two women share the same
father. . . .
"Powerful, juicy reading."
—*San Jose Mercury News*

TRAIL OF SECRETS
0-451-18774-1 / $7.50

Three women—a now successful and
married, once unwed teenage
mother; a socialite and former champion
horse-rider; and her adopted
daughter, now pregnant with a baby she
cannot keep—are linked together by
fate and circumstance.
"Goudge keeps you cheering for the
book's three women protagonists."
—*People*

THORNS OF TRUTH
0-451-18527-7 / $7.50

Continuing the story begun in *Garden of Lies* . . . The impending marriage of Rose's capable and caring son to Rachel's emotionally troubled daughter threatens to uproot a lifetime of buried secrets. Once again the two women and their families are pitted against each other . . . just as Rachel learns that her mother, Sylvie, is dying.
"A likable cast . . . Goudge's adroit handling of sex and love should keep her legion of fans well-sated." —*Kirkus Reviews*

ONE LAST DANCE
0-451-19948-0 / $7.50

The Seagrave sisters were about to come home to celebrate their parents' fortieth anniversary. Instead, they are attending their father's funeral—and their mother's trial for his murder.
"Fast-paced and intriguing . . . [a] believable depiction of a family in crisis." —The Associated Press

THE SECOND SILENCE
0-451-20273-2 / $7.50

Noelle Van Doren must contend with her
estranged husband in a bitter custody
battle over their five-year-old daughter,
while caring for her ailing
grandmother. Noelle's long-divorced
parents begin to rekindle the passion
they never truly let go, and Noelle herself
finds the courage to embrace a new
love. And three generations of women
discover just how far a mother will go
for the love of her child . . .
"Another grip-the-reader from the
popular Goudge." —*Kirkus Reviews*

Visit Eileen on-line: www.eileengoudge.com